I0712363

Tales from the Jessica Files - The First Book of LSE

Also by Punis Russi

Tales from the Jessica Files
Tales from the Jessica Files - From Bad To Worser
Tales from the Jessica Files - The Definitive Companion
Guide (One, Two, Three)

TALES
FROM THE
JESSICA FILES

-

The First Book of L.S.E.

After all, this is a love story.

PUNIS RUSSI

First printing edition 2023.

Published by Secret Freezer Publishing, LLC., PO Box 1025, El Mirage, Arizona, 85335

https://www.secretfreezerpublishing.com
https://punisrussi.me

ISBN: 979-8-9894680-5-8 (Hardcover)
ISBN: 979-8-9894680-0-3 (Paperback)
ISBN: 979-8-9894680-1-0 (eBook)

In loving memory of **Shiro Yagami**, a most excellent companion who left us too soon. You will sorely be missed, my friend.

Forward?

Punis Russi came to my attention several years ago. Few writers have a daring conversational style and can carry a unique story like PR. He opened my eyes and mind to a world far from commonplace yet convincing in every character and *tête-à-tête*.

This world opens in new and unexpected ways in every colloquy and chapter. The conversations and interactions are delightfully authentic and engaging. Knowing the origins and background makes this even more entertaining.

PR's style is far from cliche and quite unique to his stories or writing. He invites us into a world less seen and rarely experienced, allowing us to share something we would never even consider.

-The Reverend CD for **The Amalgamated Heavy**

Introduction?

Before we begin on this journey, there is something that we here at Secret Freezer Publishing wish to share about the format and structure of these stories.

You see, we view "tales" as a story. The kind of story you'd tell a friend or loved one, sharing and possibly embellishing them.

Our story has no timeline; things do happen when they do happen, but this is not a straight line. You'll just have to read all of it for the context, content, and story to come together, like a nice orange chicken sauce.

We also hope you can open your mind and read what is written, consume it for its majestic nature, and find the lost corundum... It's out there, on the other side, waiting to be found.

————————————————————————————————

But wait, there's more...

This is the story of the most regarded and influential rock band in the world, LSE (lowselfesteem), and their relationship and their importance to our most loving and wonderful couple, Punis and Jessica.

LSE holds a very, very special place in their hearts, and why wouldn't they? They knew one another, and it shows in the love they all have for one another.

We here at Secret Freezer Publishing cannot underscore enough just how important the four most excellent members of the band are to us and their families.

Little did the world know just how important they would be and how the members of LSE would become a part of their own families.

LowSelfEsteem is:
- Robert A. Smith (lead vocals and keyboard)
- Marvalious (bass)
- Arturius (guitar)
- M.T. (MegaTon) Turner (drums)

Please join us on this most fantastic journey to musical, spiritual, and emotional bliss.

Or Contents?

L1 - Or Back Backstory?

L1 one of The First Book of LSE. This week, we learn a little more about the history of the band LSE (Low Self Esteem).

Some years ago, while I was in the IT world, I came across a couple of folks who weren't there yet, but they had a feeling that one could feel.

When I started at a job as a TL, two of the folks there, brothers, as you'd expect from this story, were a part of the team I picked up. I knew almost instantly that each of them was on the precipice of something spectacular but missing that one little thing.

During my initial onboarding, I got to meet with them individually. What a fantastic venture this was. I got to ask my standard questions, but it was when I asked this very one...

"What's your hobby? What do you like to do in your free time?"

"Well, sir, I enjoy music. I play in a band with my brother..."

"Musician, that's wonderful. I appreciate a talent like that. Any other hidden talents?" And I laughed like a supervillain...

"My friend, I love the arts. I am an aspiring writer. I wish to write about things which I find very interesting. I can only hope to encourage you to do the same."

I saw their eyes light up. Both of each brother, when I told them that. And fuck, I meant it. I so wanted out of the tech world... A grossness that knew no bounds, a degeneration unfathomable, depravity knowing no limits. I'm pretty sure that's spot on.

When I spoke with them individually, the brothers Marvalious and Arturius, I learned something about myself in the process. I could see they wanted to be set free from this stupidity and become something more. Although, most all of us want that.

And yet, during the years those brothers worked for me, I've always encouraged them to keep pursuing their dreams, as I did.

———————————————————————————————————————

Several years ago, before Jessica, I had seen a local band playing"**On A Schooled Night**," and I ran into two of the guys I had come to know in such a unique way.

We talked for a bit, and they told me they felt like they needed something more in order to get "there." I took note of that. You don't tell someone that if not for a reason.

A few days later, it hit me. Fuck! I knew these two dudes and these other two dudes.

No, I wasn't worried about losing them. No, I was worried about the world missing out on them. Such musical talents, I tell you.

I texted the brothers Marvalious and Arturius. I said, "Yo. I've got a new gig for you with a couple of guys I know who are super talented. The four of you will be magnificent.

Much like Jessica's near-instantaneous replies, I get "We're in."

They met up, started jamming, and the rest is almost history. They needed one little thing to take them to the stratosphere: a manager. And I knew a guy that I knew would enhance their talents and take them there.

I texted the brothers Marvalious and Arturius with a simple message: "555-0420 - Franklin Yukon."

Now, how many years ago that was, and from that point on, they always attributed their success to me. Every single album cover, every single album jacket, every single live concert, they thanked me. It was surreal.

I don't believe they went from zero to hero because of this guy, but I've always felt that I was the nudge in the backside that got them where they needed to be. And you can only imagine the pride I felt.

So, who are the other two I met when I went to see a local band playing out "**On A Schooled Night**?"

That's hard to denote but also very interesting. Everyone here at Secret Freezer Publishing has a backstory, and they are all juxtaposed. Hell, this could be its own damn book.

The other two members are K.W. (KiloWatt) Turner's younger brother, M.T. (MegaTon) Turner. Yeah, their parents were super fucking weird. Like super ultra mega fucking weird.

But their children, and yes, there are more than K.W. and M.T., are all super fucking normal.

Since I have known K.W. for a lifetime, that is how I know his brother, M-ton.

The fourth and most important part here is, well... he's also related to another member of the SFP family. You see when Misty Clouds got married a few years back... Damn, this part of the story is involved.

Misty and her husband, Robert A. Smith, married when they were both 18, having been absolutely in love since they were kids. Misty once told me she was seven years old when she met Robert. Who introduced them?

One Alphonso Mango. Alphonso is Misty's stepbrother and a junior member of the writing team here at Secret Freezer Publishing. His current assignment is a powerhouse of a book.

Alphonso and Robert A. Smith are still incredibly close. However many years this is now, they talk daily via video chat. Their friendship has weathered many storms over the years, but they've always had each other's back. It is such a wonderful story that I hope (nudge nudge) Alphonso denotes it to all of us someday.

Why is this important? She knew right then and there that Robert A. Smith was the one. You know, that one. Her only one, his only one. The only one. Their absolution.

Magical. It's just absolutely magical.

Aside from the nudge from myself, the chief architect of LSE was none other than Robert A. Smith. He and Misty were married for a long while before LSE was even an idea, let alone something that happened.

Oddly enough, Misty was the driving force behind me introducing everyone. You see, And for fuck's sake, Misty is not Jessica. It kills me to have to note that time and again.

I've known Misty for some time now, and she is someone I took under my wing while she was a kid. She was already super talented at that point. What a phenomenal artist she was. So skilled and intelligent.

And for the fucking love of Zeus, not only is Misty (for the millionth time) not Jessica, but Misty is... is... family. I was there the day she was born. My sister is Misty's mother... Misty is my niece.

I'm so proud to have been there that day to talk and spend time with her father, my brother-in-law, Franklin Yukon. I've known Franklin for many, many years. I don't want to blow up how long ago that was, but we met in high school playing soccer. But I'll save that for another day.

I had already known M-ton and Robert A. Smith for a lifetime. So I knew how amazing they were, how wonderful those two were as humans, and just how fantastically talented they were.

Yeah, this guy, this idiot, yeah... I'm the one who had set all of this in play in a rather accidental manner. That's why LSE loved me, as they knew I loved them. I loved them all because I knew all of them, and I loved all of them as the humans they are.

They were all a part of my family, and they were all incredibly important to me. So, each member of LSE and every member of the Secret Freezer Publishing team are related in some way or another.

Every Thanksgiving, we get together at Hello Shen Go to celebrate their success and what they will build.

And just off to the side of this picture are the two who take it. Yup, Jessica and I. We got to be a part of, and therein a witness, the most amazing things in life, the things we hold dear.

I had my Jessica, and that's all that mattered to her and me. But to the world, they had LSE, and LSE had their family, all of us. Us.

L2 - Or Fargo?

L2 two of The First Book of LSE (or the band LowSelfEsteem). This week we learn where how somewhere can be everything for some.

I got a call from Franklin Yukon earlier in the day, asking me to meet him for dinner at Hello Shen Go that night, along with Jessica. And like always, I told him, "I'm in!"

Franklin and I go way, way back. As we have noted in **L1 Back Backstory**, Franklin and I are related in a most amazing way.

Franklin and I played soccer in high school, however many years ago. We weren't on the same team, but we were the same age. We played against one another twice a year for four years.

And, it was Franklin's job to mark me. Sideline to sideline. If I left the field as a sub, he was there waiting for me when I came back on.

I was honored because I wasn't a superstar here,
but like the idiot that I am, shit happened around
me.

I'm an idiot that failed forward if you will.

But I loved those games. Even if Franklin marked
me out, we would still find a way to win. He was by
far their best player. Take the two best off the field,
and some shit happens.

We became friends over the years. After high
school, Franklin went on to Eastern Fargo Business
School on a full ride. I can not tell you how proud I
was of him, in him.

Over the years, Franklin and I stayed in touch. Mind
you, and this is before the interwebs. Yeah, we are
that old. Sigh. But yeah. We'd talk on this thing they
call a landline phone often.

And then, one day, everything changed. I'd gone to
lunch with one of my sisters (you can guess which
one), and Franklin happened to come in. This was
the first time they'd met.

"Franklin, so wonderful to see you. Please, sit down and join my sister and me."

 I say sister because I'm sure as fuck not using names here. "Sister, this is Franklin Yukon. We played soccer together, perhaps against each other, while we were in high school."

Franklin was immediately smitten. I can't blame him, but more because of the person that she was, and I know that she will become.

I introduced them officially, and the rest just took off like a bottle rocket. I could not argue or sabotage this attraction. I could only wish the best for the two of them, as I now know the rest of that.

Yes, **L1 Or Back Backstory** stuff. They married a few years later, once Franklin graduated college with his Master's of Business Management. He was a smart cookie, too.

I was his best man and got to take in all of this for them, for their day. I was proud of the two of them. I loved them both. They were family.

It was one of those moments, you know, a pillar moment, where Franklin got the family thing. He wasn't Italian...

Fast forward a few years, and then... I got that phone call. The surprise and shock, happiness and joy that I experienced one spring day when Franklin had called me along with my sister, and they proclaimed to me. "We're pregnant!!!"

I was so joyous for them, so happy and proud. I mean. I was going to be a shitty uncle, much like I was a shitty brother and a shitty son. I mean to say... yeah, all that.

Some time down the road, I got that phone call. The one of "Hey, your sister is going into labor. Meet us at the Lady of the Worthless Miracle Hospital."

I laughed so hard that I nearly pissed myself.

"Franklin, where?"

"Meet us at the hospital, you dork." And he laughed just as hard as I did.

"OK, my friend. I'll see you there."

And I did. I spent the afternoon with him as he paced about, waiting for even the slightest bit of news. He wanted to be here, there, and not there, if you know what I mean.

It gave Franklin and me such a wonderful opportunity to talk and reminisce about the four years we got to play soccer against one another. It was something to take his mind off what was going on.

He had a slightly weak stomach if ya get me?

Then the doctor came out, walked over to him, and said, "Sir, you are the proud father of a healthy baby girl. Congratulations."

I caught Franklin as he fainted. I've never known, then or now, whether he was hoping for a boy or girl, but I always knew he wanted a healthy child, regardless.

And he sure did. I was invited in to see my sister, along with Franklin now that he wasn't being a pansy, to see his newborn daughter.

I remember the moment for two reasons. The first is their joy together, having created life. And the second, because my sister turned to me and said, "Punis, what should we name her?"

Emphatically, I stated, "**Misty Clouds**. What a wonderful name for such an amazing child. My sister and one of my closest, trusted friends have brought this life into our world. This is the name I would give her. **Misty Clouds**."

And in unison, I got "**Misty Clouds**. We're in."

I love them, all of them. They are my family and a part of the family that we will grow. While my sister will be in the background of this story, Franklin and Misty will always be a major part of it.

————————————————————————

L3 - Or Part ONE of Hello-LSE-Go?

L3 three of The First Book of LSE (or the band LowSelfEsteem) This week, we learn how LSE blows shit up at Hello Shen Go in a nice way.

Jessica had mentioned to me the other day that she wanted to go for a sit-down dinner at Hello Shen Go. That was in "**P4 - Dinner for Two**" of **Tales From The Jessica Files**.

That didn't turn out as we had discussed, but it turned out to be something so unexpectedly incredible. It was... was...

"Jessica, I'm sorry we didn't go to Hello Shen Go the other night upon request. If you are interested in going tonight, now, I would like to do that."

"Sir? Should we do Fashion Runway Time? I will go start the ritual as per the contract."

"Jessica, it's OK. The Department of Rules and Contracts, or DORCs for short, is aware of us missing that agreed-upon window and has graciously granted us another. And that's now. Now, now. Like now."

"Sir, are we not doing Fashion Runway Time for this tonight? And if not, what would you like me to wear to dinner at Hello Shen Go?"

Sometimes, the length of formality we go to is astonishing, but then I know the love we have for one another would permit us to do so without question. It was just love.

"Ma'am, there's no reason to get changed. I love you just the way you are. You are very, very memorable."

"Thank you, Sir. I feel like a Southern Belle..."

I started to belly laugh in a boisterous manner. It was too fucking spectacularly cute.

"Ma'am, I remember that day, in that kitchen, and..." I trailed off for a second as I thought about how stunning she was on that day so many years ago.

And I need not note this, but fuck, she was so much hotter now! She was the complete package of a human. She was very memorable, indeed.

"Ma'am, you are just everything. I love you, inside and out."

Jessica blushed. It really was adorable.

And you know adorable isn't about kids when you swoon about the things your partner does, with the emotions it brings with it totally dunking on your ass.

She made me feel like that by just thinking about her. I loved her so much, and she was just so special to me. And yes, I need a better adjective, but fuck, it's spot on.

"Ma'am, gather up what you need, and let us go. I may have a surprise for you later. But we'll see."

I did shit like that so she knew I was going to present her with a surprise, and I wasn't fucking around, but in a way that we were covered in the contract.

Folks seem to miss what a contract is from time to time. It's a legally binding document. We lived within the rules of the contract. So did anyone else who signed a contract... If they were smart.

As we exited the Rydemnow, I noted to myself how spectacular it was to watch her move and how it had been something that I took much pleasure in doing, as appropriate. When Jessica was in my presence, I would typically stare at her and her beauty.

I just loved her so much, and one day, I hoped that I could show her as much. She was just so... stunning. Not only her beauty but her personage. That was the real prize here. She was just such a wonderful human.

We stood next to one another in front of our favorite restaurant, Hello Shen Go; I let my left hand go, seeking her. And without looking, there it was... her hand in mine. That feeling, connection... It was... I... I... wow, she was just so...

"Ma'am, are you ready?"

"Sir, yes, Sir, I am. Let's go. I want the first toast, please, Sir."

"Yes, ma'am, the first toast is all yours. I love you, Jessica, there can be no doubt..."

And I trailed off. I wasn't... I just loved her so much. She was everything to me, the only thing to me.

As we approached the front door, I denoted again to Jessica, "I may have a surprise for you tonight. May..."

I knew who and what, but I wasn't about to let on to her about it. The rules... yeah, you line item sign, you own your own shit. But I knew...

We were seated at our table without delay. No, it wasn't empty, and no, we weren't more special than anyone else. Right time, right recognition.

We loved coming here, and you never knew whom you'd see and interact with and how amazing the experience would be. But I knew, I just knew.

The waitperson came over rather quickly, likely recognizing us from the plethora of times we'd been there.

"Mr. Russi, I'm so glad to see you again. Ma'am, you are resplendent as usual. I must say, your beauty is so..." And he trailed off.

No, I didn't care about his adulation here. He'd done so many times over but never rudely or inappropriately. There were wonderful humans here, which was in our top 2 places to be. I just loved them all.

I would often recall **P26 or Pre-Starter?** from **The Jessica Files - From Bad to Worser**, and the memories of the two of us from that night, Christmas Night, so many years ago. I remember the staff being so amazingly amazing.

From time to time, I'd see the gal who helped me that night, and I'd smile at her and dip my head in respect. She'd have saved us as much as anyone or anything else had. She was a part of this mashup of life.

"Jessica, my love, what would you like to drink this evening?"

"Sir, I would like a double Cromulent Vodka ginger ale with a side of lime, please, Sir."

"And you, sir?" The waitperson asked, fully knowing what I'd order. I'd never ordered anything else at all.

"I'd like the same as this wonderful and amazing human seated to my left. Thank you, sir."

I squared up with Jessica, and she did the same. No, this wasn't a showdown. This was two people in love absolutely. She was just so...

I put my hands out to Jessica, not too horribly shaky but enough so that she quickly grabbed mine, holding and massaging them, all the while smiling at me. She was just so fucking fantastical. She was everything.

"Ma'am, thank you for holding my hands and making me feel safe in your sphere of influence. I love you, ma'am, there could be no doubt. You are..."

And the waitperson returned, two Cromulent Vodka ginger ale's in tow, filled to the brim as we like them.

Jessica and I looked at one another, smiled, turned to the waitperson, and together said, "Thank you, sir. Can I have another?"

We both giggled like children. Our waitperson obliged and stated, "Sir, I know your toast, and I will toast you that toast if not to be rude."

I smiled, knowing some of what would come to pass tonight. "Yes, please, sir."

The waitperson pulled a small bottle of Cromulent Vodka out of their pocket, cracked it open, and noted to us:

"Sir and Ma'am, here is to the eve of the day which will never come, and, Sir and Ma'am, here is to retreat to ease the pain."

They offered out their mini bottle. We all clanked in the middle and killed our respective drinks. It wasn't the first and wouldn't be the last, but it was most memorable indeed.

After we finished, the waitperson took our empty glasses and headed off to attend to other customers before eventually coming back with the next round. It wasn't a problem, no, not at all.

"Jessica, my love of all loves that have ever loved, I may have a surprise tonight for you. You see..."

And there it was, that screeching noise. I looked up to see the two folks that worked for me. Sure, this was just before they blew up, but I was proud nonetheless.

I stood up, pushed my chair away enough to turn, and said, "Marvalious and Arturius, how wonderful for y'all to be here on this most wonderful night."

I extended my hand to Marvalious and then to Arturius to shake their hands. This was meant to be formal; I promise you that.

I started without hesitance, "Brothers, most awesome; please allow me to introduce you to my most excellent life partner, Jessica.

"I know I've gone on and on about her over the last few years, but I wanted you both to meet her. She's really astonishing."

As if in stereo, they state, "Sir, your adulation of Jessica does no justice to her. She really is memorable."

I saw the brothers quickly look at one another, then back at me. As I've learned, it was a lightbulb moment for them and for LSE.

"Jessica, please allow me the pleasure of introducing you to the brothers Marvalious and Arturius. As you know, one half of the super band of LSE."

I know... Not everyone in the world, let alone in this restaurant, knew who LSE was. Not yet. But they would come to know them, but not like I did.

I think Jessica was starting to melt down before I interceded to bring her back. And you know what's going to happen here.

And then, this party got started. We all peered to my right as the doors swung open. There were two folks there, two folks we all knew. Well, minus Jessica for now.

They turned and stared at the table. No, this wasn't a bad thing. No, it was most excellent. Exceptional. Amazing, All that and a bag of chips.

Towards me more than anyone else, these two gents approached. I stood. I knew these guys, man, how I knew them.

"M-ton, such a pleasure to see you, my friend." And we hugged a special friend's hug. I'd known him since he was a kid. His brother, K.W., was my closest friend.

"M-ton, where's your older brother, my homie?"

"Sir, he'll be here shortly, along with another of our friends." And he grinned that grin.

I turned, and I extended my arms to one Robert A. Smith. He was the architect and, well, much more backstory in **L1 Or Back Backstory**, so no spoilers here. I mean, I'll try.

"Robert, where's your most awesome wife?"

"Sir, she'll be here in a bit. We might need a bigger table, Sir."

"Sounds good. Robert."

I waved down our waitperson since we'd added a couple of folks for our small table. They knew they knew.

"Sir, we'd like to move to a larger table, please. It's the six of us and..."

Robert interjected, "Sir, add four. My wife and father-in-law will hopefully be joining us shortly, along with a couple of our friends... We need them here... All of them."

I smiled that smile of smiles, that smile of one hundred billion trillion smiles. That one of joy. It's one of the very few non-Jessica smiles I think I've ever had.

I scanned the table and noted to our waitperson, "OK, table for ten then?"

They smiled back. "On it, Sir."

As I stood there, I could only wonder what would come to pass as I knew from the tone of Franklin's voice, the specific phrases and words he used (see **P31 Or Interviewed?** from **Tales From The Jessica Files - From Bad To Worser** for that shit.)

But that's not the point here as I've known Franklin for a very long time. No, the point was how memorable this was going to be.

————————————————————————————

L4 - Or Part TWO of Hello-LSE-Go?

L4 four of The First Book of LSE (or the band LowSelfEsteem) This week, we get the amazing conclusion to this wonderful event.

Fuck how I loved coming here, being here, at Hello Shen Go. And here I was, with my Jessica, at our favorite place, with my favorite people, to be adding some more favorite people. I was in heaven.

Other than the formalities, I'd have had my hand in Jessica's hand the whole time. I knew. I knew this was a lot, and I could tell based on how quiet she was. I didn't want that. I wanted her to open up.

I turned to my left, where she'd be for this life and the next, and whispered into her ear, "I grant you off the record, **Jess**."

I called her that, knowing how much she didn't like it, but I granted her off the record for a very special reason.

"Don't worry, **Jess**. I need you here, with me, right now. I need you to be in this moment, frozen in this moment with me.

"You are everything to me, **Jess**. Everything. I need you here with me. I know that I will pay a heavy cost for this, but that is just how much I love you. I really need you here with me, my only love."

And boom, just like that, Jessica was back here with all of us, with me. I could feel her power again. It was just so wonderful.

Jessica became involved in the conversation, which allowed me to slowly fade out of it, taking it all in. I knew this could be a great dinner with our family, all of it.

I just knew, and not because I was the orchestrator of it. I mean, come on now... this guy isn't that smart. Or is he? The actual answer is no. This guy is a moron.

And just like that, the doors swung open again, and there they were—those two. I knew them both. I'd known one far longer than the other. But we'll save that for another day.

Robert A. Smith stood up nearly instantly, with M-ton, Marvalious, and Arturius shortly cascading thereafter. Now, this was something to see. I mean, again, I knew all of them, but...

After a wonderful hug from his lovely gal and a handshake to the gentleman, Robert A. Smith turned back to the table and said:

"Please allow me to introduce the table to my wife, my love of all there is to love, Misty Clouds, and to my most awesome father-in-law, Franklin Yukon. I am so thankful you are both here.

"This is going to be a most spectacular night, I promise."

I looked on and took in what was going on. Sure, I knew, but I wanted to be there, with them, with Jessica, for this moment. I wanted to be frozen in this moment.

I stood and turned. First, I got a loving hug from Misty Clouds; what a superbly talented artist. The talent there... and I trailed off in my mind.

Misty turned to Jessica, gave her a huge hug, and they whispered to one another for a bit, a very special conversation. You know, a very personal one. It was touching.

And then I got a warm handshake from a longtime friend, Franklin. I've known Franklin for many, many years.

And then the doors swung open again. This time, it was personal. OK, personally, more than anything else in this personal story.

And in walks two folks, two more folks I've known for a lifetime, as did M-Ton and Robert A. Smith.

Like a dart, they walked over to the table. M-ton was the first out of his chair, hugging his older brother K.W. and then his longtime pal Alphonso Mango.

Robert A. Smith was up shortly thereafter, and Robert went straight for Alphonso Mango, someone so dear, important, so... his best friend.

This was something to take in. It'd been some time since I'd seen those four together; it was super wonderful.

But then, it was my turn. I stood and pushed my chair back once again as the two approached me. It was such a moment.

I extended my hand and stated, "Alphonso, my friend, I'm exceptionally glad to see you. It's been a spell."

"Yes, Sir, it has been. I'm sorry, you know the project I'm working on is..."

"Alphonso, I know it's your first book. You are going to do a fantastic job, I promise. I'd not asked you to write that if I didn't believe in you, my friend.

Alphonso pepped up a little, smiled, and stated to me, "Thank you again, Sir. I'm thankful to have your support and for your willingness to help others ."

I smiled, and then I turned, squaring up to K.W., my homie, my lifelong tag team partner. A supervillain with me, forever with me.

I just reached out and got a loving, friendly, I haven't seen you in person in a spell hug. This was the first spot where I thought I'd lose my shit.

"I miss you, my brother," I said.

"I've missed you too, my brother."

We smiled that smile, homies, till the end.

K.W. turned from me, reached his hand out to Jessica, and stated, "Ma'am, it's been far too long. I miss your cooking, especially the orange chicken. Damn!"

Jessica smiled and lovingly matter-of-factly stated, "K.W., you are always welcome for dinner. You only need to ask me ." Complete with a wink.

I knew Jessica knew who all these folks were, all of them. The band, the wife, the father-in-law/manager, the bestie, the protege... but she'd never met any of them aside from K.W. and her step-niece, Misty Clouds, and tonight was going to be so special, so...

Robert A. Smith started things up. "Everyone, all of our family, all of our loved ones. I've asked everyone here tonight to this lovely restaurant that I will claim as our own."

Robert looked over to me, winked, and continued, "I'm sorry, Punis. This is _our_ place now." At the same time, gesturing circularly to indicate the entirety of the group.

I knew exactly what Robert A. Smith meant, and I may have blushed. I was so proud. You have no idea.

I gave Robert A. Smith a head nod. He knew I knew, and he knew I was all in. I was already family, long ago family, but that's covered in **L1 Or Back Backstory**.

I'd never let my hand off of Jessica. I knew she was taking it in, not panicking at this point. While I wanted her to be engaged, I didn't want her to be one.

Misty turned to Jessica as she scanned the table and said, "Jessica, my friend, it's so wonderful to see you again. It's been a spell, and you are indeed memorable. You are just so astonishing, and we all know this to be true."

I was so taken aback by all of this. Sure, I knew something was going down. I'm just not sure what that was. I mean, wait, no, it would be more accurate to say that I had no idea what was going to come to pass.

Franklin had called me earlier in the day and asked
for Jessica and me to be there tonight. I told him, as
I'd told him a million times, if not once in the past...
"I'm in."

 I know that we were all in a state of suspense. Our
waitperson came over and asked for drink orders,
and everyone at the table ordered: "Cromulent
Vodka Ginger Ale with a slice of Lime, please." Now,
that was ridiculous.

It was one of those times when I felt like this was...
It was that time when my life was over as if this was
sending me off. I mean, I know that I wasn't about
to be Soylent, but still.

Robert A. Smith continued, "My family, LSE, we all
love our family. So why are we all here **On A
Schooled Night**?"

Robert's eyes darted over to me before darting
quickly toward M-ton and returning to his
comments.

"Franklin, would you do the honors and hand out
the first party gift to each person at this time?"

Franklin nodded. I knew the nod. It was one of
those "Fuck yeah, I'm in!" That happiness of
something you believed in, that feeling.

And there it was, their debut album, in 180-gram
vinyl, signed by each member of the band with
unique messages as tributes to each member of the
family here.

Yeah, I know. I don't sign my books when I give
them out. It's because I want that one signed copy
to mean so exceptionally much that I... Fuck? I know
I'm not high, but damn, I was up in there.

But wait, there was more. Of course, right?

Robert A. Smith stated to the table, "La Familia;
there were only eight copies of this album made.
Marvalious, Arturius, M-ton, and myself, with
Franklin on hand, providing evidence.

"Franklin, could you please hand that gift out at this time?"

"Yes, sir. On it.

Robert A. Smith continued, "We took the only existing mold for this album, and we smashed it into eight pieces. One for each of us. There'll never be another copy of "Absolute Time" on vinyl anywhere, evah, ah-gain.

Each piece was encased in an acrylic case, which was the same size as a vinyl album. On top of that, each piece had a certificate of authenticity that had been signed by the band.

"Oh... But wait, there's more..." Robert A. Smith said.

My goodness, he'd already maneuvered two mic drops tonight. What could he possibly have to top them? I mean, seriously, I'd known tonight was going to be special, just not special like that.

Robert A. Smith continued, "I hope you like your gifts, but there really is one more. I'll ask my bandmates to help out here and hand out the last one.

"My friends and family, this is something that only the five of us knew about until this moment. We want us all to be, as Punis would say, Frozen in the Moment."

I blushed once again.

And the band handed out another album, which was odd, given they had only pressed one and destroyed the mold. I was a little perplexed.

And then M-ton came over to me, handing me an album whose cover was just breathtaking. I was just so blown away.

Robert A. Smith turned to me and stated to the table, "Sir, this is to honor your journey, with K.W. documenting it. It is such an intense and emotive book."

Robert was talking about The Other Side by K.W. Turner. It hurts to have been to that place, that other reality, without my Jessica.

And with that, I felt a tear roll down my right cheek. Oh, Jebus, dude, get your shit together. We can't allow us to blow up here, now, can we?

"Punis, this album is titled "Sapphire." We all know that story, and the four of us wanted to show you just how important you are to us.

"You, Sir, are the reason we are here today. Without you, none of this would happen. None of it. Thank you, Punis, for helping us achieve what we have and for what we will be."

I sat there stunned as I looked at this most wonderful album in my hands. This was so spectacular, and maybe this was my send-off.

Franklin came over to Jessica and handed an album to her, which was signed by each member of LSE. That was the only copy that was signed, a tip of the cap to me.

"Jessica, thank you for being here with us tonight. You are family now."

With that, Franklin then gave her a loving kiss on the top of her head, the way you would to someone who was in your tribe, signifying that his statement was, in fact, honest, loving, and truthful.

"But wait, there's one more party favor for the table," denoted Robert A. Smith.

Robert A. Smith had a smile ten miles wide. "We have eight copies of each album and the fragments. We have given our family six of those eight copies. So what to do with the others?

"Franklin suggested, and the four of us instantly and emphatically agreed, that we should auction off each of those pieces for charity.

"We, LSE, will cover all of the fees, shipping, etc., for these treasures. We will ask each of you to tell us what charity you would like those donations sent to, on your behalf and that of the bands.

"Where would we be if we didn't share some of our heart and soul with those who make it pump? All of them, all. It is so incredibly important to give back."

K.W. stands, surveys the table, and comments, "I don't know about y'all, but I heard that Punis was going to pick up the check as a way to give back." He winked.

Alphonso was the next to stand, winking over to K.W. and affirming, "That's what I heard earlier, too. That makes it a fact."

And then the table busted out laughing. I was oblivious to what was going on around me as I was still in shock. I couldn't get a grasp on the events unfolding.

I continued to stare at the copy that was handed to me. And yet still, even still at that time, I did not know what was going on.

———————————————————————————

At the end of the night, it was just the boys and me at the table, the gals having hit the restrooms, and Franklin had gone to get a RydemNow for Misty, Robert A. Smith, and himself.

K.W. and Alphonso Mango were right behind Franklin, knowing they'd wait their turn so the others could leave first.

The four of them, Robert A. Smith, M-ton, and the brothers Marvalious and Arturius, staring at me, stated as a team, "Sir, we'd like you to write the lyrics to a song we have in mind. It's called "Memorable". It's about Jessica and your love for her.

"We all know that your love for her is... It's unfathomable to calculate just how much that is. But would you write us something to immortalize her in that?"

I was further blown away if that was even possible. I fell into my seat, not completely sure of what the fuck was going on ...I wanted to cry again, like full-on tears of joy pouring out. I was probably rather glossed over.

My long-time friends, my direct reports, wanted me to write the lyrics to a song about my Jessica. I mean, I'd only published four moderately not unacceptable books and still was trying to gain some footing.

Good lord, how I wanted out of this shit in the IT world. It's what I've encouraged the brothers to do as well. But I knew how amazing the brothers were, and I knew just how amazing M-ton and Robert A. Smith were.

They had the most excellent leadership in place with Franklin Yukon. And they all had the loving support of their family, all of us. Us.

——————————————————————————

Jessica and Misty came out from the restrooms. Jessica walked directly to me, leaned down, and gave me a loving and emotive kiss on the cheek.

"**Dude**, thank you for bringing me here tonight. And **Dude**, thank you for making me a part of the night. And **Dude**, could I go back on the record now, please?"

"Yes, Jessica, we are back on the record."

"Sir. I love you. Thank you for this experience tonight." She looked down at the two albums and the album fragment that she was clutching. Their debut album, "<u>Absolute Time</u>," and their follow-up album, "<u>Sapphire</u>," and she started to tear up.

"Jessica, my love, they all love you. When I told the brothers about that conversation, you know, the one, they were enthralled. They must have liked your response as I did."

That conversation, as a note, is in reference to **P39 or Cherry Pie?** Of **Tales From The Jessica Files - From Bad To Worser.**

I smiled at Jessica. I knew that it would be an honor, a pleasure, to write a song about her, per the request from Robert A. Smith, M-ton, and the brothers Marvalious and Arturius.

I know that it'll take a few days before I come back to earth, but I do have her here with me to ground us.

This was the start of a new chapter of our life. The one with our family. All of them. It was so...

"**Dude**, you ready already?" Jessica said to me in the most sarcastic of ways. It was like when we were at **The Ice Hole** in **P34 Curling? of The Jessica Files - From Bad to Worser.**

I know we were on the record, but I couldn't resist a boisterous laugh. "Ma'am, yo ass betta call some boddy!!!" WWF's New Age Outlaws again, lol.

We both giggled like the morons that we were. I was blessed to have her in my life and to share mine with her. We were blessed before tonight, but tonight, our family had just grown.

———————————————————————————————————

L5 - Or Frozen?

L5 five of The First Book of LSE (or the band LowSelfEsteem). This week, we learn how cold shit is.

This is the tale of the "**Frozen in Fargo**" album and show where **Memorable** debuted in an empty stadium, just like they liked it.

Since the album was hitting shelves after the show, no one knew what was on it. It was a mix of **Absolute Time**, **Sapphire**, and a couple of new songs.

One of which is **Memorable**. That was the encore. Just one song. And that one song cemented their already massive success and turned them into the world's most important, influential, and revered band.

The album was released on April 20th, 2020, at 4:20 PM local time.

————————————————————————————————

The four of them stood there on the stage. Robert A. Smith was the lead singer and a keyboard wizard. To his right was five-string bassist Marvalious, and to Robert's left was guitarist incredible Arturius. Behind all of them was MegaTon, M.T. Turner, the drum kit master.

They stood there on stage, waiting for the queue to come from the Teleprompter that indicated that their pay-per-view was on. They were live and about to show the world something so incredible and so special that it was by all accounts impossible.

LowSelfEsteem was about to officially blow up. They would blow up there in Fargo, North Dakota, where Franklin Yukon, their manager, had gone to college. He had gotten a master's in business management from Eastern-Fargo Business School. See **L2**. It's important to note for a reason.

"Gents, we are 30 seconds out," said Robert A. Smith as he turned to his bandmates and asked everybody to huddle at the drum kit.

Once there, Robert noted, "This is our time, and we've got some folks in our family to do right by tonight. All of them. All.

And with that, they turned back their attention to their spots, and when the counter hit zero, and the red light came on... this was their time.

Robert stood there and waited a few seconds before stating, "We are LSE, low self-esteem. And we are going to play tonight for you on pay-per-view a combination of our first and second albums plus a sneak peek at a brand-new song that nobody has heard yet, not even our Manager...

"Oh, there's one more thing about tonight... Swing the cameras around, please."

And as the cameras turn, they show a completely empty stadium, just like one of their absolute favorite bands, <u>Greenland Floyd</u>, had done at Krakatoa some years ago.

Then the camera swung back to Robert A. Smith, and he stated outright.

"It's time for..." Robert A. Smith proclaimed, **"TREAAAAAADDDDSSSS!!!"**

And there was that. Off they went, performing the most exceptional show that would later be pressed on vinyl for their third album, entitled <u>Frozen in Fargo</u>.

After 90 minutes of extremely impressive and excellent sound and light experience, it felt as if so much energy and emotion had been combined into a tiny slice of time. It was time again for Robert A. Smith to talk to those watching.

Robert A. Smith got on the microphone and said, "Thank y'all for watching. We need a 10-minute break, and then we've got something <u>Memorable</u> for y'all."

Little did any of them know, including their manager, Franklin Yukon, what was going to come to pass with the playing of the last song of the night as their encore.

That song was a very special song that they had requested me to write for them about Jessica and about my love for her. No spoilers, but **L6** of **The First Book of LSE**.

After said 10 minutes, the boys came back and took their equipment, got set, and Robert A. Smith stated to the cameras, "This song is a little long, but holds an incredible amount of emotion and energy. This is <u>Memorable</u>."

And off that song went. This was the true start of LSE and the start of something so astonishing, amazing, transcending, so...

As I sat there on my couch and watched this spectacle, knowing that I had written the lyrics for them to encapsulate my love for Jessica, I couldn't help but think about the fact that this woman that I love, just so absolutely, the person of my attention and affection, sitting right here, next to me, was unaware of the song that they were listening to, and falling in love with, was about them.

And never at any point was Jessica aware of this up until **L6** of **The First Book of LSE**. I made sure of it, and so did the boys and Franklin. It was an agreed-upon oral contract, and I would have it no other way with the people that I knew and trusted, those whom I had grown up with, and those who have worked for me.

When I did tell Jessica, it was something special, just like her.

L6 - Or Memorable?

L6 six of The First Book of LSE (or the band LowSelfEsteem). This week we learn about things that are memorable.

▌▌ Jessica, a friend of mine, has offered me some tickets to fly international first class, which I want us to do."

"But, Sir? Please, I don't want to travel, Sir..."

And I cut her off. "Ma'am said friend is LSE. They offered us some tickets to travel first class around the world. LSE, they love us as I know we love them."

I chuckled to myself that this was an anniversary gift for us to celebrate ourselves and the tremendous success of LSE over the years, however many that is now.

It was a flight around the world, über first class. We're talking easily $250,000 for this travel package. And that was a very special gift for us.

When I spoke with Franklin Yukon that day, he told me of this gift. I was blown away, just absolutely blown away. And I didn't argue because of how much of a supporter I was of them, of him, well before day 1.

And never once did I ever expect any compensation. It was for the love of music, the gift they had.

They knew the level of dedication I had for them. Before they were a thing, I knew them all as individuals, wonderful humans.

Something that Jessica wouldn't know until she read this back, backstory, as we've never revealed it to anyone. At all.

But I've gotten permission because of the gift I wanted to give Jessica. I wrote "Memorable" about her, per their request for something extraordinary.

I just loved her so much and in such an intense manner. She was my Ma'am, the only Sir she'll ever have.

She was everything to me, the only person who meant anything to me. Yes, she was memorable indeed. Enough so that, well... I never told her about this, knowing full well it was her favorite song.

Jessica was something so special, and she was so absolute to me.

I wrote her the lyrics for the song that we love absolutely, her favorite song, to be performed by our absolutely favorite band. What kind of guy does something ridiculous like that?

I know the answer: this guy. This guy loved that girl in such a way. She was just so... special. Just mind-blowing.

"Ma'am, how many times have you read through the jackets of LSE albums?"

"Sir, hundreds of millions of times, if not once."

"Jessica, do you know who wrote Memorable?

"Sir, LSE did... Why do you ask?"

"Jessica, please go grab that album jacket, you know, "Frozen in Fargo," and let's talk about it."

And then boom, in a jiffy, she was back-album in hand, "Frozen in Fargo." And I asked her, "Jessica, tell me who wrote Memorable."

She replied, "Strings by LSE and Words by ptr, Sir."

"Ma'am, who is ptr?"

"Oh my God, Sir!!! Did you write Memorable for me???

"Jessica, if you make that loud screeching sound like a teenager again, there'll be a heavy toll." ...

Jessica was seemingly unfazed by my statement. I'm sure it registered, but I could tell she wasn't all here right now.

"Sir, OMG!!!! I'm going to melt down like Chernobyl. Oh my God, Sir... " And she trailed off, falling to her seat, blown away.

I continued to look at her, and I wanted her to emote. It was so incredibly important that I reached her in such a manner.

"Ma'am, you damn well know I could call any of them and ask them to verify the statement. They are big fans of us, as we are of them."

I can't believe I finally let that one go. From time to time, I would use the word to accurately describe her, to represent her.

But I know that I've never even come close to mentioning any of that to anyone, let alone to her. I don't believe I ever even alluded to it: my goodness, the scandalousness of such a notion.

"Ma'am, I hope that you will someday know just how much I love you and how much you mean to me. You are everything I could ever want in a mate or partner.

"Jessica, you are so fucking special to me. Damn, I don't think I can ever tell you how much, let alone show you."

"Sir, you wrote the most famous song in the world for me? You wrote that for me, for?"

"Jessica, you know this to be true. You know I was trapped in a world without you, the pain and suffering." And she cut me off.

"Yes, Sir. I'm so sorry, Sir. I just.................. I never knew that Memorable was about me!!!"

"Bitch," and I giggled. God damn, I loved this woman with everything I had ever had, all of my essence. She was just so fucking amazing.

"Jessica, I could not imagine a life without you. I once lived in that. I died in that. I didn't have the strength to go on without you. You are the power, the regenerative force that keeps me alive."

I slightly turned away from Jessica as I knew my emotions were starting to blow up on me.

"Jessica, without you, not even LSE could save me, save the boys. You know this to be true."

With that, I saw Jessica stand up and walk towards me out of the corner of my eye. She was seemingly upset. I knew why, and I felt the same way.

"Jessica, I love you. I love you so much as not to tell you I wrote our favorite song, knowing it would taint our love for their music. I could not allow it. I demanded as much from them.

"I can only hope you come to know how incredible they are as humans, especially when they come for dinner."

I turned and looked at Jessica, expecting a Homer Simpson drooling moment. But I did not get that. I got something else, something much different.

I got Jessica, my Jessica, staring back at me like she'd been frozen in ice. Unable to move or function. I knew what it meant.

She was in the initial phases of a panic attack, and I had to pull her out of that place the way she had done for me.

I knew she needed an <u>Antidote</u> to pull her back, back to me. I did not want this spot to blow up with such an amazing reveal of something so dear to us, our hearts.

I immediately ran to her, pulled her into me, and whispered into her ear, "I grant you off the record, **Jess**."

I called her that, knowing how much she didn't like it, but I granted her off the record for a very special reason.

"Don't worry, **Jess**. When they come for dinner, I'll cook."

And like that, she came back to me as I knew that she would. "But, Sir, that would be unfair. Why would you want to punish them like that?"

I laughed strong and hard as I stood there, holding her lovingly close to me, like the hug of all hugs on Christmas Eve day so many years ago.

"Thanks, <u>Dude</u>. I really fucking needed that, and while I don't appreciate you using that name, I surely appreciate you granting me off the record.

"<u>Dude</u>, that was super fucking fantastic. I love you, Punis.

"Thank you, Sir.

"How about we make some Cromulent Vodka/ Zevia's, have a big shot of Sour Zed, and relax a little while you tell me more about how you will give them food poisoning by cooking for them!"

That was followed by her laughing super fucking hard, as she would often do before **P1o ten Collar** from **Tales From The Jessica Files**.

"Ma'am, that sounds like a wonderful idea. What say we..."

And Jessica cuts me off. "Sir, Could I go back on the record? Please?"

"I grant you on the record."

"Jessica, I want you to know that I never told you because I knew how much you would love this song when I wrote it, and as I said earlier, I did not want to taint that.

"I just knew that this song would be so incredibly special for us that I just..." And I trailed off for a second, trying to prevent myself from tearing up.

"I've told you many times over, in all of the years we've been together, however many that is now, that I could only hope to show you how much I love you one day."

"I asked LSE to drop that album on that day and at that time, as you would expect from them.

"I never told you because I wanted us being there at that place by ourselves, with The Reverend CD, to remind you now of what that means.

"I love you, Jessica Gabriela, my most excellent wife, my most excellent sub. I must tell you that this was the gift I gave you on our wedding day, as my gift to you so many years ago.

"That was the gift of absolute love, Jessica. And now, perhaps, <u>you know just how much I love you</u>."

————————————————————————————————

ACKNOWLEDGEMENTS

The **Reverend CD** - You are the one constant in my life, my most excellent friend. I write this after I've nearly had my own Chernobyl-level meltdown when I hadn't spoken to you in a couple of days.

You could hear it in my voice when we spoke on the phone. So could your wife, as I was freaking the fuck out.

To anyone who reads this, yes, the **Reverend CD** is the only person I have spoken with daily over the last 6+ years and is still the only reason I bother to write, especially when I feel like there's no point.

Aside from apathy, sir, you are so important to me as a human and have had such a tremendous impact on my life. You've given me ideas, thoughts, pointers, adjustments, suggestions, and on and on. You, sir, are just so important to me as a human that I do not believe I can articulate that in the totality of my life, past, present, and future.

———————————————————————————

Dr. Jasmin - You continue to be a major player in my life in so many incredible ways. Please know that I am writing this part after we went to dinner, and I specifically told you that the event made me feel like an adult. Only you could do that, Dr. Jasmin

You are a great friend who knows so much about me and with whom I have so many loving and fantastic memories.

And who would I be if I left out something far beyond horrific, and you came to console me because of my fucking BLEEP ass knees.

We slept that night as best as we could, given the pain, shuddering, the scariness of having to bear witness to it.

But we slept that night together as two humans, hand in hand, as only the most amazing of friends could do.

And for those who read this, yes, we did sleep together that night, hand in hand, not letting go, regenerating one another's energy, and bringing me back as a human.

That night showed me so much about myself, about you, and about our friendship that I'd be remiss not to include it in this story.

I owe you so much, Dr. Jasmin - Thank you for sharing time with me while we've been getting to know each other once again as the humans we are and helping me fit in.

You really are astonishing. And my love for you is stronger.

————————————————————————————————

Good Sister - I will only ever have two sisters.

I know that when you come to see me... fuck my BLEEP ass knees! Thank you for showing me the path to redemption and always being positive, encouraging me to do the same.

We've all got our shit, and I learned how to own it from you. Thank you for that, amongst the millions of other things a big sister would do for her little brother.

I love you, **Good Sister**, as I do **Bad Sister**. The three of us are the exception to our parents and their madness. Some of us know this more than others... ahem, **Bad Sister**... 🙂

I love you, **Good Sister**, for being a force of reason throughout my life. You've always been loving, kind, and spectacular. That is what we were taught by those no talent ass clowns.

But wait, there's more as you once again have saved me, saved the boys. I write this with tears in my eyes, knowing just how instrumental you have been in my life.

I owe all that I have in my life to you, **Good Sister**. I mean that with the most sincerest emotions possible. <u>Sho level</u> emotions. Without you, I would not have survived long enough to be trapped on The Other Side, let alone this time and date.

Good Sister, I will only ever have two sisters.

————————————————————————————————

Bad Sister - I will only ever have two sisters. **Bad Sister**, you've never done me wrong. EVER. And I remember that email asking me why you were a "BAD" sister.

And I know I chuckled a bunch when I emailed you back.

Bad Sister, you've been detached from my life, as I have from yours, your families. But I know that you love me as only a middle older sister could do. You are, unknowingly, such an incredible force in my life.

No, it's not because you are clearly provably crazier than I am. No, it's more than that. It's that you are one of three, and there'll be none other.

I know you took care of me as a child for ever so long. Through the sicknesses, hospitalizations, and surgeries, all before I was ten years old. You always made sure to take care of me.

I cannot do justice to my perception of your love for me above and beyond your taking care of me. Time and again, you, **Bad Sister**, took care of me.

Where the fuck would I be without you? Oh, I know... I'd never made it there.

<u>I love you</u>, **Bad Sister**. And I will only ever have two sisters.

———————————————————————————————————

The Great Daniel L - Sometimes, it's hard to articulate your feelings about another person when it comes to the emotional toll that one pays with another.

You know the toll. You know the physical pain I am in. And yet, you continue to be a rockstar who listens to these stories, one chapter at a time, one month at a time.

One of the reasons I enjoy seeing you is to tell you the latest, knowing that, at some level, you are happy for me and very proud of my turning the pain that I have inside of me into something less worse.

More than all the others here, I wish I'd listened to you.
Time and again, I wish I had listened to you. It is
perhaps one of the biggest mistakes I've ever made in
my life, and perhaps I wouldn't be trapped here.

.

————————————————————————————————

Fry - I miss you, my friend.

I really could use the phenomenal amount of power that
you had and would give to me. But I understand.

You were with me, there on The Other Side. Reading
about it, well... I wish you could, but I know I'd never be
able to in your position.

I do greatly miss you being a such an important part of
my life. You've had a tremendous amount of impact on
me, and you know that it'd take a bit to spell all of it out.

Sure, the 1 a.m. phone calls, some years ago, sucked and
were shitty of a friend who clearly is a moron,
completely incapable of caring for themselves.

And yet, you cared for me and about me for so long.
Sometimes, I could listen, and in others...

I really do miss you, my friend.

————————————————————————————————

Mrs. B -You've been there for me to the point where, as a human, today, when I'm writing this, is Saint Kane's day. And when we chatted, you'd have had a shit-tac-ular day. IIRC, your watch said 96% stress levels.

I mean, you know I love your husband, dog, oh, and you, in such a way that I wanted you in my life. And many years ago, you asked about being friends. I jumped on that shit.

No, fuck you, anyone who thinks otherwise. Already had former co-workers who were NTACs. They don't get free copies, bitches.

Mrs. B, you are the one that called me that night. Only you. And while my friends were loving and supportive, you are a fucking rockstar.

————————————————————————————————

Dr. G - Thank you for everything you continue to do for me as a human, continuing to transform me into a less screwed-up version of me. See, I didn't say fucked up.

I do enjoy chatting about these stories, the wacky ideas I come up with, and how, from time to time, they make sense on a grander scale.

I feel as if, since I started this train wreck in March of '22, you've heard more about my ideas than any other person and likely all parties combined, including the Reverend CD.

Thank you, **Dr. G.**, for your generosity and love and for showing me the level of care you can give another person. Without you, I'd be far more broken and destroyed in life.

————————————————————————————————————

Kirk -We've known one another for 20+ years now, and not until I wrote this, I never thought I'd call you Kirk anywhere and at any time outside of the bedroom. Evah, again...

And yet, aside from the ridiculousness of calling you Kirk and my love for you as a friend, you've always been you—a friend and a balance.

I know that I'm a pain in the ass, ask Larry, and that my dedication is incredibly deep; also, see Larry. I hope one day he lands here (after learning how to read).

While, as humans, we don't always align, I listen to your thoughts and beliefs, and I have acted upon them repeatedly.

I should have listened about getting married... 🤭😂 j/k,
she's a good human, and I mean no disrespect to her.
But "ex-wife/husband" jokes, man, they write
themselves.

———————————————————————————

Dana -I've told you, privately and in print, just how
important you are and will always be to this story.
Without you, none of this would have happened. You
know this to be true.

I hope one day to show the world just how true the
story is, how true our friendship is, and just how much
fun it was. And when I do, you will be the first to know.

You are one of the smartest, most loving, honorable,
and most fantastic humans I've ever known. There's a
reason that you and the **Reverend CD** are in the spots
you are.

It's not FLA. No, it's more spectacular than that. You see,
without the both of you, none of this happens. I
specifically am stating the <u>two of you</u>. Both of you are
the most important people to this story, to my life
during that time and onwards.

To open and close the most heartfelt acknowledgments
I can give, you both kept me alive, moving forwards or
at least sideways.

Dana, I really do listen to the voicemail from time to time. The sincerity within and a friend's love towards another can be heard. It is the exceptionalism of who you are and why I will always love you as my friend.

Once again, **Dana**, thank you for helping me try to get over the goal line in this story, all **145,262** lines of it. Yeah, that's the number of lines in our chat history. All of it between friends.

That is why I sought your approval on certain content. You expressed your feelings, and I respect that. Period.

I wish I would have listened better and not ended up...

<u>Oh, and would it kill ya to do another cookie massacre silliness for Festivus this year?</u> 😊

————————————————————————————————

And lastly... <u>**Sapphire**</u> -**Hey**! I shopped there because of you! And now I'm trapped at the DMV. HELP!

While this is the end of this story —>

Their story has only just begun...

Lx - Or Another Special Gift

This is another special gift (or curse) from Punis to the three people who will buy this masterpiece. This is from a coming title in TJF2.

———————————————————————————————

A quote from Punis during "**A Kiss Destroyer**" presser session:

I have a hard time understanding that, as an author, my job is to write books and sell them. Well, what if I want to write books and have them published, and I don't give a fuck if anybody actually reads them?

What if I want to write books that make people think? What if I don't want to give them the answers like they are toddlers? What if I want people to read this and understand it because they want to understand it?

There's always a hidden corundum waiting to be found, like a game that you cannot imagine yet because you are not yet capable of seeing it now.

Do I need to put a warning label on my books? The one that is labeled "T.H." for the thinker? That is not what and why I write.

I write in hopes that one can open their mind, dispel all belief, and take in the content, having opened their mind, heart, and soul to something that would challenge all three.

And that is the story of this guy.

I have long written with the philosophy that I am writing for myself, and I don't care if other people read it or even like it. And why is that? It is straightforward. It's a single word, an idea, or a unique concept. Yeah fuck it, I don't care about it... apathy.

I have had a lot of pride in what I've written in blog and book formats. I still have a lot of pride in my writing, but no fucks given whether or not others do.

I've worked with editors who got it and those who didn't, but I wasn't ever bothered by what they did; it was always about the linguistics of what they said I wrote.

You see, linguistics is essential to understanding the words in the meanings of what has been written or is being transcribed to you, let alone audio linguistics when talking with another person or persons.

Linguistics will give you the actual truth about what is being said and allow you to examine the content and context of what is said...